PAUL STEWART

An Elephant Never Forgets

CORNELSEN ENGLISH LIBRARY

Cornelsen

An Elephant Never Forgets
Paul Stewart

Verlagsredaktion
Susanne Döpper

Umschlaggestaltung
hawemannundmoch, Konzeption und Gestaltung, Berlin

Titelbild
Shutterstock/Johan Swanepoel

Illustration
Kay Dixey, Linda Grant Agency

Technische Umsetzung
Harald Kertz

www.cornelsen.de

1. Auflage, 13. Druck 2021

Alle Drucke dieser Auflage sind inhaltlich unverändert und können im Unterricht nebeneinander verwendet werden.

Druck: AZ Druck und Datentechnik GmbH, Kempten

ISBN 978-3-464-06824-3

PEFC
PEFC/04-31-2260

PEFC zertifiziert
Dieses Produkt stammt aus nachhaltig bewirtschafteten Wäldern und kontrollierten Quellen.
www.pefc.de

CONTENTS

CHAPTER ONE

It was so hot outside that you could cook an egg on the road. There was no wind. There were no clouds. The air was dry; the ground was as hard as rock.

In the small two-room house, it was almost as bad. The little window kept the bright sun out, but it was still terribly hot.

Arif was lying on his bed. He felt ill. He felt weak. He felt very, very old.

'Time is passing so quickly,' he said. 'The end will soon be here.'

His mouth was dry. He wanted some water, but his glass was empty.

'Sukari!' he called. 'Sukari ...'

But then he remembered. His wife was shopping in town with their oldest daughter, Sara. The house was as empty as his glass. Arif was alone.

'Oh, well,' he said quietly. 'I must wait. They'll be back soon.'

He listened, but heard nothing. It was too hot for the people and the animals. The village was quiet. Suddenly, Arif felt very lonely.

He looked up. There was a black spider with short legs on the ceiling over his head. It was walking slowly from the wall with the door to the wall with the window. Arif watched the small animal's long, long journey, and thought of his life.

'*My* long, long journey,' he said quietly. 'From the little baby that I was, to the old man with white hair and weak body who

I have become.' He smiled. 'I have seen so much. So many changes.'

He remembered the country when he was a boy. White men governed then. Independence first came when he was a young man. He danced in the streets on that day, he was so happy. It was 12th December, 1963. He could remember how the people laughed and shouted on that day.

'*Harambee*!' President Kenyatta called. 'Pull together!'

'*Harambee*!' everyone shouted back.

Arif never forgot that day – or the day after. Friday 13th. It was the last time that he saw Anraak.

'But where are you now, old friend?' he said. 'Where have you been all these years? My best friend. Where are you, Anraak?'

Arif closed his eyes and remembered the day when he and Anraak first met. It was on Arif's twelfth birthday. He was small then, with black hair and bright eyes. At the time, Anraak was only six months old, but he was already bigger than Arif.

This was not as strange as it seems, because Anraak was an elephant.

CHAPTER TWO

When he was a boy, Arif lived with his mother, father, two brothers and three sisters in a little hut, in a little village, in the centre of Kenya. Arif was the youngest child.

His father had a small farm, and everyone in the family helped with the work. They grew fruit, vegetables and maize; they had twelve goats and some chickens. The family was not rich, but there was almost always enough food to eat.

On Arif's twelfth birthday, his father got up before the sun. He went quickly and quietly into the children's bedroom and across to Arif's bed.

'Come,' he said. 'You are twelve today. You and I are going hunting together.'

Arif smiled. His older brothers often went hunting with their father, but Arif always had to stay at home with his mother and sisters. But not any more. Now, at last, his father thought he was old enough to go with him.

'What? Just you and me?' asked Arif. He couldn't believe his ears.

'Just you and me,' his father replied.

'YES!' Arif began to shout – but his father put his hand over the boy's mouth.

'Don't wake your brothers and sisters,' he said.

'OK,' Arif whispered. 'Sorry.'

His father smiled and took his hand away. 'Get up,' he said. 'I'll make breakfast.'

Arif jumped out of bed, washed himself quickly outside, put his clothes on and ran to the kitchen. He sat at the table. His father turned from the fire and smiled.

'You are not usually so fast,' he said.

'Today is special,' said Arif. He began to eat his bread and drink his tea as quickly as possible.

His father laughed. 'Slow down!' he said. 'We have all day before us.'

But Arif couldn't slow down. He was too excited. He was going hunting with his father: just the two of them. And for Arif, that was the best birthday present in the world.

'What will we hunt, father?' he asked. 'An elephant?'

'No, Arif,' he said. 'I have never killed an elephant. There is no reason to kill an elephant. You cannot eat them and they are not dangerous. Elephants are our friends, my son. You know that.' He stood up and walked to the door. 'An elephant never forgets, Arif. Remember that.'

'Yes, father. Sorry, father,' said Arif quickly. 'But what will we hunt?'

'We will hunt a gazelle – a small gazelle,' he said, and smiled. 'Remember, we must carry it home!'

CHAPTER THREE

At six o'clock, Arif and his father left the house. Arif quietly closed the door. He had their bag of food on his back; his father was carrying their water. Both of them had a gun over their shoulders.

'Have we remembered everything?' asked his father.

'Y ... yes,' said Arif. 'Food, water, guns ...'

'Come on, then, my youngest son,' said his father. 'Let's go and hunt.'

Together, they left the village with its huts and houses, and its small church. They walked across the small fields and went onto the wide African plains. The sky was red. The tall trees looked black against the giant sun that was coming up over the horizon. The sounds of wild animals were all around them.

'Are you frightened?' his father asked.

'No,' Arif lied.

His father looked at him. 'It is all right to be frightened,' he said. 'The plains are dangerous. If you are a little frightened, you will also be careful.'

They walked on. Mile after mile. Hour after hour. Dry and brown, the land needed water. But the rains were late this year. There were no clouds in the sky, and the sun shone, hot and bright.

Arif's father drank a little water. He gave some to his son.

'Thank you,' said Arif. 'Is it still far to go?'

'No,' answered his father. 'We're almost there. We'll stop at those rocks. Over there,' he said and pointed.

Arif stopped and looked at the rocks – as large as buildings – where the mountains began.

'But it's miles away!' he said.

'It's not so far,' said his father and smiled. 'You cannot see it from here, but there is a water-hole near the rocks. Because the plains are so dry, there will be a lot of animals there. Gazelles, zebras, giraffes. Believe me, Arif. Let's go.'

As they walked towards the rocks, Arif's father told Arif about his plans. Arif listened carefully. He didn't want to do anything wrong. He wanted his father to be proud of him.

'There is a tree near the rocks,' said his father. 'First, we will eat, then we'll rest in the shadow of the tree. Later, when it is not so hot, we will hide behind the rocks and wait. The frightened animals will soon forget us. They'll go back to the water-hole and start to drink again. It is then that we'll choose our gazelle ...'

'Yes,' said Arif. 'And tonight we will cook it over a big fire, and everyone in the village will come and eat with us.'

'A *small* one!' Arif's father laughed. 'Don't forget, Arif. We are looking for a small one.'

They walked quickly towards the rocks. The sun climbed in the sky. Slowly, slowly, the rocks came nearer.

'There are holes between some of the rocks,' Arif's father went on. 'Small holes – just big enough for a gun.'

'But will the animals smell us, father?' asked Arif.

'Today – on your birthday – we are lucky, Arif,' he said. 'The wind is coming from the east. The animals will not smell us. And if we are careful, they will not see us or hear us – until it is too late.

CHAPTER FOUR

Neither Arif nor his father arrived at the rocks. After half a mile Arif heard a strange noise.

'An-raak. An-raak. An-raaaaak!'

Arif stopped. 'What's that?' he said.

'An elephant,' said his father. 'A baby elephant.'

They walked towards the noise. Large birds flew round and round in the sky in front of them.

'Vultures,' said Arif's father. 'There must be something dead near here.'

He ran towards the area where the noise came from. Arif ran behind him. One after another, the vultures flew down and landed. Suddenly Arif understood why. A large female elephant was lying on the ground. She was dead. The vultures were all around her.

Next to her was the baby. A six-month-old elephant with hair on its head and back, and a black star above its eyes. It was touching its mother with its trunk. Then it lifted it, and trumpeted loudly.

Arif ran towards them. The vultures jumped back and watched angrily. The baby elephant walked away and trumpeted louder. Arif looked at the dead elephant. There was blood around her mouth.

'What happened?' he said.

'Poachers,' said his father angrily. 'They were here not long ago.'

'But ...' Arif began. He didn't understand. Why were the mother elephant and her baby not with the herd? Why was the mother elephant dead? Why was there blood around her mouth?

'They kill the elephants for their ivory,' his father explained. 'If we are not careful, all the elephants on the plains will disappear. And why? Because ivory brings money.' He looked at the baby elephant. 'And without mothers, the babies die.'

'Die?' said Arif.

'They need milk,' said the father.

'But we have milk in the village,' said Arif. 'Can we take the baby home with us?' he asked. 'Can we, father? It will be safe with us. And when it is big enough it can return to the plains.'

Arif's father shook his head. 'Elephants are wild animals. They are not ...'

But Arif was not listening. He moved towards the baby elephant very slowly. The elephant watched him.

'Don't be frightened,' Arif whispered.

The elephant lowered its head, but did not walk away.

'I want to help you,' Arif said, 'not hurt you. Come with me and I will look after you.'

For a few seconds the elephant did nothing. Then it looked at its mother, lifted its trunk and trumpeted.

'An-raak!'

When it looked at the boy again, Arif was sure that the animal was crying. 'Come on,' said Arif. 'Come with me. Let's go home.'

Suddenly the elephant made a decision. It put out its trunk, blew the boy's hair – and then took his hand. Arif's father was so surprised that he couldn't speak. He turned and began walking. Arif and Anraak followed him. Together they returned to the village.

Arif looked at his father. 'I will call him Anraak,' he said.

CHAPTER FIVE

A baby elephant is always hungry. It eats too much for one family alone. Fortunately, the other people in the village liked Anraak, too. They thought that the elephant with the black star on its forehead brought luck.

Every day they gave powdered milk to Arif, who mixed it with water. Seven litres, five times a day, Anraak drank. Thirty-five bottles a day! He grew big and strong.

But the people of the village were happy. They fed Anraak, and he protected the village from thieves and wild animals.

One night, a group of monkeys came into the village. They were hungry and were looking for food. Anraak saw them. He lifted his trunk and trumpeted until the men and women of the village woke up and chased the monkeys away.

The next morning, to say thank you, the people of the village brought Arif's father twice as much powdered milk as normal for Anraak.

On another night, a thief arrived. It was dark and windy. The thief went quietly from house to house. He took money and jewellery and was just leaving the village when Anraak saw him.

He trumpeted and ran after the man and caught him with his trunk.

Anraak was a star!

'He has saved us again,' said a man.

'Anraak is the best elephant in the world,' said a woman.

'We love you, Anraak,' said the children.

Arif felt very proud. Anraak – *his* Anraak – was so important. Before he came to stay with them, the village was sometimes a dangerous place to live. Now, it was safe. He climbed onto Anraak's back and raised his arms.

'Hurray for Anraak!' he shouted.

'Hurray!'

But as the years passed, things changed. Anraak grew older and bigger – too big for the village. He drank more and more milk. He began to eat, too – the grass for the goats, the corn for the chickens, the food the people of the village grew for their families, the fruit they collected from the trees.

Anraak never went far from the village but, as he grew older, the plains became more interesting for him. He often stood alone and watched quietly. He looked at the trees and bushes, at the grass that came and went with the rains. He raised his trunk and smelled the air. There were lions out there, gazelles and zebras – and other elephants.

He could smell them. He could hear them. Sometimes he saw them, too. And when he trumpeted, they trumpeted back to him.

'Come with us,' they called.

But Anraak could not leave the village. It, and not the wild plains, was now his home.

Then one night, two weeks after Arif's sixteenth birthday, a hungry lion – old, alone and too old to catch food – came into the village. It was looking for an easy meal, a slow meal: it was looking for somebody to eat.

Anraak charged at the lion angrily. Surprised, the lion ran to the left. Anraak lowered his head and charged again. This time, the lion ran to the right. Anraak raised his trunk, trumpeted and charged a third time. At last, the lion ran away – there was blood on its shoulder.

Because of Anraak, the village was safe again.

But the people of the village did not know this. They did not see the hungry lion. They saw only the fields that Anraak destroyed when he was charging here and there.

The men of the village visited Arif's father. They were all very angry.

'The elephant must go,' said one. 'It destroyed all my corn.'

'And all my vegetables,' said the second.

'And all my fruit,' said the third.

'But he protects the village,' said Arif's father. 'For four years, no animal has stolen our food and no thief has stolen our money.'

'There is no food to steal,' said the first man. 'Anraak eats everything.'

'And we have spent all the money on milk,' said the second.

'The elephant *must* go,' said the third.

Arif listened sadly. He knew it was true. Anraak was now too big for the little village. That evening, he went to his friend and spoke to him.

'Anraak. You need more than milk now. And the village does not grow enough for you and us. I'm sorry but ...' he began to cry. 'You must leave. You must return to the plains.'

From far away came the sound of the wild elephants. They trumpeted loudly, again and again.

Anraak looked at Arif for a long, long time. Then he lifted his trunk and trumpeted.

'Oh, Anraak,' said Arif. 'I will never forget you or how I found you. And when I am a man I will become a ranger. I will catch the ivory poachers and put them all in prison. I will. I promise ...'

Arif stopped. He could not speak. He was crying too much. Anraak blew warm air down his trunk and into Arif's hair. It was what he always did when the boy was sad. Arif looked up and smiled.

'You must go now,' he said.

The elephant pulled his trunk back, turned around and walked away. He went out of the village and onto the plains.

He followed the sound of the wild elephants: he didn't look back. Arif watched sadly as his friend disappeared into the darkness.

'Goodbye, Anraak,' he said, 'And good luck.'

CHAPTER SIX

On his bed in the hot bedroom, Arif remembered how sad he was when Anraak left home. He opened his eyes.

The spider was still walking slowly across the ceiling. Arif closed his eyes again. The memories continued.

When he was eighteen, Arif also left home. His father was dead and the farm now belonged to his oldest brother and his family. They lived there with Arif's mother. The other brothers and sisters had to find their own homes. Together they all worked on the small farm.

Arif was happy to leave. The farm was too small for so many people, and he didn't want to be a farmer all his life. He still remembered his promise to Anraak. He wanted to catch the ivory poachers and protect the elephants. So he found work with the rangers in the nearby national park.

At first he did all the dirty jobs – but he was happy. Later, the other rangers gave him more important work. He looked after the baby animals who were without parents. He looked for poachers with the other rangers at night. He also learned how to drive a jeep. Soon Arif was driving groups of tourists onto the plains.

For five years Arif did this. He knew the places where the lions liked to sleep, the water-holes where the elephants liked to eat and drink. He knew where the big cats liked to hunt.

The tourists loved him. And he loved his job. But something still made him sad. During all this time, Arif did not see Anraak – not even once.

Arif's best friend, Kenneth, was also a ranger. He told him all about Anraak one evening when they were driving back to the rangers' compound.

'I found him on the plains on my twelfth birthday,' he said, 'and he lived in the village for four long years. But he grew too big. The men of the village said he must go. Then, one morning, he followed a herd of wild elephants and disappeared. That was the last time I saw him.' Arif looked at Kenneth. 'I hope so much that the poachers haven't killed him. Oh, Anraak,' he said. 'I hope that you aren't dead.'

'You and Anraak were good friends,' said Kenneth.

'We were best friends,' said Arif. 'Do you know if anyone has ever found a dead elephant with a black star above its eyes?'

Kenneth shook his head. 'The poachers kill so many. We are losing the fight, Arif ... But perhaps your elephant has been lucky.'

'Yes,' said Arif. 'But he lived in my village for so many years. I'm afraid he likes people too much. He doesn't know that some are dangerous.'

'Perhaps he remembers what happened to his mother,' said Kenneth. 'They say an elephant never forgets.'

'That's what my father told me,' said Arif sadly. But Anraak's forgotten *me*.'

CHAPTER SEVEN

A week later Arif was driving across the plains again. This time he was alone. He was still thirty kilometres away from the rangers' compound when he heard a strange noise from the back of the jeep. He stopped and got out.

'Oh no!' he shouted when he saw the flat tyre. 'I'll have to fix it without any help.'

He looked around. It was already dark. Arif was feeling frightened. But that was all right! He remembered his father's words. *'The plains are dangerous. If you are a little frightened, you will also be careful.'*

'Yes,' said Arif, as he continued to look round. 'Be careful and you'll be fine.'

Suddenly Arif heard a sound from the bushes. His heart stopped. Something was there.

'It is probably just the wind,' thought Arif.

But then he saw them: two cold, yellow eyes, which were staring at him. The next moment, the bushes moved and two more eyes appeared. Then another two. And two more …

All together there were five lions – five big, strong lions. They opened their mouths, and Arif saw their dangerous yellow teeth.

'Oh, help,' he whispered.

He knew that he was in trouble. Usually lions did not attack people, but the rains were late again and the animals of the plain were all far to the south. The lions were hungry. Very hungry.

'I don't want to be their next meal,' Arif thought. 'I must get my gun.'

But how? The gun was in the jeep.

'If I move, the lions will attack,' thought Arif. 'If I *don't* move, the lions will attack. What can I do?'

Arif wanted to disappear – but that too, of course, was impossible. He felt hot and cold. His mouth was dry. His legs shook.

'Perhaps, if I scare them, they will go,' he thought.

Arif opened his mouth and screamed. He screamed louder and louder and louder. And when he finished, he screamed again!

The lions were surprised – but not scared. They did not run away. Instead, they made a circle around the jeep. Now it was not possible to get his gun. Arif looked at the lions. The lions looked at him.

'Please don't attack me,' he said. 'My body is thin. There is not much meat for you.'

But the lions started to walk towards him. Arif knew that this was the end.

'I'm too young to die,' he thought. 'There is so much I still want to do.' Then he shouted, 'Oh, help! HELP!'

CHAPTER EIGHT

Suddenly, Arif heard the sound of loud trumpeting. The next moment a large, heavy elephant with long tusks – and a black star above its eyes – crashed through the bushes.

'Anraak!' Arif shouted. He was excited to see his old friend, of course, but he couldn't believe that he was there again – after so many years and at such a lucky moment.

Did the elephant know he was in danger? Did he always follow him? Was he always nearby?

Maybe. Maybe not. It wasn't important. Anraak was here now: big and strong, and very angry!

With his head down, Anraak hit one of the lions with his tusk, and threw it over his shoulder. Terrified, the lion ran away. There was blood on its neck. Anraak attacked the second lion, which was standing by the jeep. He put his head down again and charged. The lion could not move quickly enough and, the next moment, it had a bad injury on its back.

'Yes!' shouted Arif.

Anraak looked round for the other lions. They were running away into the darkness. Anraak lifted his trunk high and trumpeted loudly, again and again.

Arif watched him. He felt happy and sad at the same time. He walked towards him.

'Oh, Anraak,' he said. 'I am so happy to see you again. And happy, also, to be alive. Thank you, Anraak. I needed help, and you saved my life. But … where were you all those years? he asked. 'Why didn't you come back to see me before?'

Anraak looked at him and touched the young man's face with his trunk.

'Look at me, Anraak,' said Arif. 'I don't know if I want to laugh or cry.'

The elephant raised his trunk and blew warm air into Arif's hair. Arif looked up and smiled.

'Anraak, my old friend,' he said. 'I called and you came. You saved my life.'

Anraak blew air into his hair again. Arif laughed. He remembered the night when the monkeys came, the night when the young elephant caught the thief. He remembered the night when Anraak went away …

But now Anraak was back. The question was, did he want to stay?

'If you must go, don't go yet,' Arif said. 'Please.' He stroked Anraak's trunk. 'Stay here while I fix the flat tyre. And be careful! Maybe the lions will come back.'

And that is what Anraak did: he waited until Arif could drive the jeep again. Then, when he was sure that his old friend was safe, he raised his trunk, trumpeted – and walked away.

Arif jumped out of the jeep and shouted after him. But Anraak did not stop. He disappeared into the darkness again. He did not look back.

Sad, but not surprised, Arif climbed back into the jeep and drove away.

CHAPTER NINE

Arif arrived at the rangers' compound at nine o'clock. His friend, Kenneth, was waiting for him.

'What happened?' he said. 'I thought you were in trouble.'

'I was,' said Arif. 'But an old friend came and helped me.'

'An old friend?' said Kenneth. 'Who?'

Arif smiled. 'I'm hungry now,' he said. 'I'll tell you everything that happened after dinner. Let's go and eat.'

When Arif came to the end of his story, he looked down at the table.

'He protected you from the lions,' said Kenneth.

'Yes,' said Arif. 'Oh, I know you probably don't believe me,' he said, 'but ...'

Kenneth smiled. 'I believe you,' he said. 'I've heard other stories about elephants who helped people. You're lucky to have an elephant for a friend, Arif.'

'I know,' said Arif. 'The lions were so dangerous. I thought it was the end for me.'

'But Anraak came to you when you screamed and called for help,' said Kenneth.

'Yes,' said Arif.

'Maybe he remembered your voice.'

'Maybe,' said Arif. 'But why was he so near to me? Was he following me? Was he watching me?'

'I don't know,' said Kenneth. 'I'm sure that no elephant has ever done that before. It was probably just chance.' Kenneth laughed. 'But it's not important. He came, he chased away the lions and he waited there until you fixed the jeep. And, Arif, you are still alive!'

'That is true,' said Arif. He looked at Kenneth. 'But ...'

'But what?' said Kenneth.

'Anraak's tusks are so big now,' said Arif. 'They are at least a metre long. If the poachers find him, they will kill him for the ivory.'

'You're right,' said Kenneth.

'He's in danger,' said Arif, 'and I want to protect him. But how? What can I do?'

Kenneth looked at Arif. 'Maybe there is an answer,' he said.

'What?' asked Arif.

'The new head-ranger has had an idea,' said Kenneth. 'He plans to find the elephants, shoot them with a tranquilliser dart and then cut off their tusks while they are sleeping. He hopes that if the elephants have no ivory, the poachers will not kill them.'

Arif said nothing. He knew that the plan was sensible - but Anraak was his friend. 'That's impossible!' he said at last. 'I cannot do that. How will he live without his tusks? How will he fight without them?'

'It's your decision,' said Kenneth. 'A poacher with a gun is the biggest danger he will ever meet.'

'I know,' said Arif sadly. 'I know.'

CHAPTER TEN

The head-ranger's plan went well. During the following months the rangers took and burned the tusks from more than a hundred elephants. But Anraak was not one of them.

It was just before Christmas that Arif met Anraak at last. On the day that Kenya celebrated its independence from Britain, Arif was in Nairobi with some of the other rangers. They had waited for this day – when Kenya became a free nation– for so long, and they were so happy. The whole day was like one long party. Late at night Arif and the other rangers drove back to the national park. The weather was hot and very dry for this time of year. Arif noticed that only one water-hole which they drove by still had water in it.

'That is where I shall look for Anraak,' said Arif to his friend Kenneth. 'Tomorrow. And if I don't find him there, then I won't look for him any more.

The next day Arif and Kenneth drove back to the water-hole. They arrived as the sun was going down and parked the jeep behind a rock. They watched and waited.

Zebras and gazelles came to drink. Some lions came and went again. But there were no elephants.

'It's getting dark,' said Kenneth. 'Let's go.'

'I want to wait for ten more minutes,' said Arif. 'I ...'

Suddenly there was a noise and an elephant appeared. It was a large elephant with a black star above its eyes.

'Anraak,' Arif whispered.

Anraak was very thirsty. He walked into the water-hole and drank the brown water greedily. He did not see the jeep or the rangers.

Kenneth turned to Arif.

'Now, you must decide,' he said.

Arif looked at Anraak sadly. The black star above his eyes went up and down as he drank. The long ivory tusks shone. Arif thought about the poachers with their guns ...

'OK,' he said. 'We'll do it.'

Without another word the two men got out of the jeep and walked quietly towards the elephant. Arif carried the gun and the tranquilliser darts. Kenneth carried the saw.

When they were near enough, they lay on the ground. The wind was coming from in front of them, so Anraak could not smell them. Arif lifted the gun to his eye.

Suddenly, Anraak heard something. He looked up and saw the two men. Arif looked at Anraak. Anraak looked at Arif and at the gun. Then the elephant lifted his trunk and trumpeted. The noise was sad.

'Why?' it seemed to say. He seemed to know what was happening.

'I'm sorry,' said Arif quietly. 'You'll be angry now. But perhaps one day you'll thank me.'

With these words, he fired the gun. The tranquilliser dart hit Anraak in the neck. He walked slowly from the water-hole. The strong elephant began to look weaker and weaker. Suddenly, he fell to the ground. The next moment, he was sleeping.

Together, Arif and Kenneth ran to the elephant. Anraak stayed still. Arif fell to his knees and kissed Anraak on his black star. He turned to Kenneth.

'We must be quick,' he said. 'Anraak is so big. He won't sleep for long. Give me the saw.'

Arif cut through the first tusk easily. The second tusk was more difficult, because the tip of it was in the ground. Arif was careful. He didn't want to cut the elephant's mouth.

'Faster!' said Kenneth. 'He's beginning to move.'

'I'm ... doing it as fast as I can ...' Arif said as he sawed.

Finally the job was finished. Then, with the two heavy tusks in his arms, Kenneth returned to the jeep. Arif stayed where he was. Anraak moved again.

'Come on! Let's go!' he said to Arif. 'He'll be very angry when he wakes up.'

Arif knew that Kenneth was right. But he couldn't leave without an explanation.

'We did it because of the poachers,' he said. 'Oh, Anraak. You know that they killed your mother. I didn't want them to kill you, too. Do you understand?'

Anraak moved again. His eyes opened. Arif didn't know what the elephant was thinking. He felt frightened. Perhaps they were not friends any more: Anraak was still a big, strong – and very dangerous – wild animal.

'I have to go,' said Arif. 'And please don't forget, I did it because I love you.'

Perhaps Anraak understood Arif's words. Perhaps not.

The years went by. Arif got married and had six children who grew up. His children got married, too, and Arif became a grandfather with many grandchildren. But in all this time Arif never saw his elephant friend again.

CHAPTER ELEVEN

Arif opened his eyes again. The room was hotter than ever. He was thirsty, but there was still no water in the glass next to his bed.

'Sukari,' he called weakly. But his wife was still shopping at the market. Arif lay back on the bed. The spider was almost at the other side of the room. It was not moving.

'Yes,' thought Arif. 'I have had a good life, an interesting life. My country now has independence. I am a husband, a father and a grandfather. I have saved many elephants from the poachers.' He smiled. 'And I have been happy.' He stopped. 'Oh, Anraak,' he said. 'Why could you not forgive me?'

Suddenly, Arif heard a noise outside. Then the door opened and Arif's wife ran in.

'What is it, Sukari?' he asked.

'Oh, Arif. I am so frightened! An elephant has followed me from the market. It's enormous and its tusks ....'

'Tusks?' said Arif. So it wasn't Anraak.

'Yes, tusks' said Sukari. 'They are short, but they are strong.'

'And are they sharp at the tips?' asked Arif.

'Someone cut them a long time ago.'

Arif sat up. He felt excited. 'Does this elephant have a star on its head?' he asked. 'A black star. Here,' he said, and touched his own forehead above the eyes.

'Yes! Yes!' said Sukari. 'Have you seen him before?'

'Of course, I know him well!' said Arif. He had cut off Anraak's tusks to save his life, but he was not proud of what he had done and had never told his family about his old friend. 'Where is this elephant now?' he asked excitedly.

'Outside,' said Sukari. 'But you must stay here. He looks dangerous.'

But Arif was not listening. He got up from the bed, walked quickly to the door and went outside. And there was Anraak, black against the bright sun.

Once again the memories came back to him. He remembered the time when he and Anraak first met, out there on the plains, when he was young and the elephant was small and sad. He remembered the village where he was born – the monkeys, the lions, the thieves – and all the milk that Anraak drank. And he remembered the night when he shot Anraak with the tranquilliser dart and sawed his tusks off.

'Oh, Anraak,' said Arif quietly. 'You have become the biggest elephant that I've ever seen.'

As Arif watched him, the elephant lifted his trunk and trumpeted loudly to the sky. Then he walked towards the old man, put out his trunk and touched him softly on the hand. Arif looked into the elephant's sad eyes.

'At last,' he said, and tried not to cry. 'You have forgiven me.'

Anraak looked back. Suddenly, he lifted his trunk again and blew warm air into Arif's hair. Arif laughed.

'Welcome back, Anraak,' he said. 'You were almost too late ... I am old and weak, but now I can die a happy man.'

CHAPTER TWELVE

When Arif finally went into the house, Anraak stayed outside. And when Arif closed his eyes for the last time, Anraak was still there.

Anraak lifted his trunk and trumpeted softly and sadly to the silver moon.

'An-raak! An-raaaaak!'

Then, with his head down, he returned to the plains. For the second time in his long, long life, there were tears in Anraak's eyes.

There were many people at Arif's funeral: his family, men, women and children from the village where he lived and from the village where he was born, and also the rangers who he once worked with. Kenneth, who now lived in Nairobi, travelled through the night to be there.

'He was a good friend,' he told Sukari. 'My best friend. We had many adventures together.'

'I know,' said Sukari. 'He often talked about you.'

Kenneth smiled. 'But I was not his best friend,' he said.

'No? Who was?' asked Sukari.

'His best friend was called Anraak,' said Kenneth.

'The elephant,' said Sukari.

'Yes,' said Kenneth. 'Anraak saved Arif's life once. Then Arif decided to try to save Anraak's life. He cut off his tusks so that the poachers would not kill him for his ivory. He wanted to protect him, but Anraak never forgave him.'

Sukari shook her head. 'He did forgive him,' she said. 'In the end.'

'How do you know?' asked Kenneth.

'He came back when Arif was dying,' she said. 'They became friends again.' Anraak remembered him.'

'So it is true what they say,' said Kenneth. He smiled. 'An elephant never forgets!'

VOCABULARY

A

above [ə'bʌv] über
across [ə'krɒs] über, durch
alive [ə'laɪv] am Leben
all together insgesamt
at last [ət 'lɑ:st] endlich
at least [ət 'li:st] mindestens
(to) **attack** [ə'tæk] angreifen

B

from the back of hinten in
(to) **be born** geboren sein
(to) **become** [bɪ'kʌm] werden
blood [blʌd] Blut
bush Busch

C

(to) **carry** ['kæri] tragen
(to) **catch** [kætʃ] fangen
ceiling ['si:lɪŋ] Decke
chance [tʃɑ:ns] Zufall
(to) **charge (at)** angreifen
(to) **chase away** [tʃeɪs] verjagen
(to) **celebrate** ['seləbreɪt] feiern
circle ['sɜ:kl] Kreis
cloud [klaʊd] Wolke
(to) **come up** (hier) aufgehen
compound ['kɒmpaʊnd] Siedlung
(to) **continue** [kən'tɪnju:] fortfahren, fortsetzen, fortfahren
corn [kɔ:n] Mais
(to) **get dark** dunkel werden

D

darkness ['dɑ:knəs] Dunkelheit
decision [dɪ'sɪʒən] Entscheidung
(to) **drive by** vorbeifahren
during ['djʊərɪŋ] während

E

enormous [ɪ'nɔ:məs] massiv, enorm
enough [ɪ'nʌf] genug
even: not even once ['i:vən wʌns] nicht ein einziges Mal
excited [ɪk'seɪtɪd] aufgeregt
(to) **explain** [ɪk'spleɪn] erklären
explanation [eksplə'neɪʃən] Erklärung

F

farmer ['fɑ:mə] Bauer, Bäuerin
female ['fi:meɪl] weiblich
fight [faɪt] Kampf
finally ['faɪnəli] schließlich, endlich
(to) **fire** ['faɪə] abfeuern, abschießen
(to) **fix** [fɪks] reparieren
flat tyre [flæt 'taɪə] platter Reifen
forehead ['fɒrɪd] Stirn
(to) **forgive** [fə'gɪv] vergeben
fortunately ['fɔ:tʃənətli] glücklicherweise
funeral ['fju:nərəl] Bestattung

G

gazelle [gə'zel] Gazelle
goat [gəʊt] Ziege
grandchild ['græntʃaɪld] Enkelkind
grass [grɑ:s] Gras
greedy ['gri:di] gierig
grew up: (to) **grow up** erwachsen werden
grew [gru:]: (to) **grow** [grəʊ] wachsen; anbauen

H

head-ranger [hed'reɪndʒə] Oberwildhüter/in
heart [hɑ:t] Herz

heavy ['hevi] schwer, stark
herd [hɜ:d] Herde
(to) **hide** [haɪd] verstecken
high [haɪ] hoch
(to) **hunt** [hʌnt] jagen
hut [hʌt] Hütte

I
impossible [ɪm'pɒsəbəl] unmöglich
independence [ˌɪndɪ'pendəns] Unabhängigkeit
instead [ɪn'sted] stattdessen
ivory ['aɪvəri] Elfenbein

J
journey ['dʒɜ:ni] Reise

L
(to) **land** landen, aufsetzen
lay: (to) **lie** [laɪ] sich legen
lying: (to) **lie** [laɪ] liegen
(to) **lie** [laɪ] lügen
(to) **lift** heben, anheben
(to) **lower** ['ləʊə] senken
luck [lʌk] Glück

M
maize [meɪz] Mais
(to) **get married** heiraten
market ['mɑ:kɪt] Markt
memory ['meməri] Erinnerung
mile [maɪl] Meile

N
nation ['neɪʃən] Nation
nearby nahe gelegen; in der Nähe
neck Hals

O
once [wʌns] einmal

P
(to) **park** [pɑ:k] parken
perhaps [pə'hæps] vielleicht
plains [pleɪnz] Ebene
poacher ['pəʊtʃə] Wilderer
powdered milk [paʊdəd 'mɪlk] Milchpulver
prison ['prɪzən] Gefängnis
probably ['prɒbəbli] wahrscheinlich
(to) **promise** ['prɒmɪs] versprechen
(to) **protect** [prə'tekt] schützen
proud [praʊd] stolz
(to) **pull together** zusammenhalten
(to) **put out** ausstrecken

R
(to) **raise** [reɪz] erheben, hoch heben
ranger ['reɪndʒə] Wildhüter/in
reason ['ri:zən] Grund
(to) **rest** ausruhen
(to) **return** [rɪ'tɜ:n] zurückgehen/-kehren
round and round [raʊnd] rundherum

S
(to) **saw** [sɔ:] sägen
saw [sɔ:] Säge
(to) **scare** [skeə] erschrecken
(to) **seem** [si:m] scheinen
sensible ['sensəbel] vernünftig
shadow ['ʃædəʊ] Schatten
sharp [ʃɑ:p] scharf
shone [ʃɒn]: (to) **shine** [ʃaɪn] scheinen
(to) **shoot** [ʃu:t] schießen
shoulder ['ʃəʊldə] Schulter
silver ['sɪlvə] silbern
slow down! ['sləʊ daʊn] langsamer, nicht so schnell
(to) **smell** [smel] riechen
(to) **smile** [smaɪl] lächeln
sound [saʊnd] Geräusch, Ton
spent: (to) **spend** ausgeben
spider ['spaɪdə] Spinne
star Stern

(to) **stare** [steə] anstarren
(to) **steal** [sti:l] stehlen
still (immer) noch; ruhig
strange [streɪndʒ] seltsam
(to) **stroke** [strəʊk] streicheln
strong [strɒŋ] kräftig
surprised [sə'praɪzd] überrascht

T
terrified ['terəfaɪd] erschreckt, voller Angst
thirsty ['θɜ:sti] durstig
threw [θru:]: (to) **throw** [θrəʊ] werfen
tip Spitze, Ende
(to) **travel** ['trævəl] reisen
tranquiliser dart ['træŋkwəlaɪzə ˌdɑ:t] Beruhigungspfeil
trumpet ['trʌmpɪt] trompeten
trunk [trʌnk] Rüssel
tusk [tʌsk] Stoßzähne
tyre [taɪə] Reifen

V
(to) **visit** ['vɪzɪt] besuchen
vulture ['vʌltʃə] Geier

W
(to) **walk on** weitergehen
water-hole ['wɔ:təhəʊl] Wasserstelle
whole [həʊl] ganz